THE YEAR 2123

OJAS AGRAWAL

Made with ♥ on the Notion Press Platform
www.notionpress.com

Contents

Preface

This is my first book and I am very excited for this.
Actually, I got an idea to write a book when I was
sitting idle after completing my school exams.
I was waiting excitingly for vacation and as it started, I
wrote it.
THANK YOU

Acknowledgements

Special thanks to
Dr Sarvesh Agrawal (Father)
Mrs. Anita Agrawal (Mother)
Ms. Sarvanshi Agrawal (Sister)
For encouraging, supporting, and giving me new and
creative ideas to write my first book.

ONE

HERE THE JOURNEY BEGINS

After a decade of sleepless nights, I had finally built a time machine! There are four options on The Time Machine: skip ten years, fifty years, seventy-five years, and the maximum of hundred! But... how did I build The Time Machine?

It was a relatively simple task. In 2013, I discovered an old piece of paper with the main secret written on it in my new house's storeroom. The four parts are scattered all over the world; there is no hint in the paper about the parts; only the names of those parts are written on the paper. The four parts are the battery, the long special wires, and the two main secret parts of The Time Machine: Jingzheittingyuming and Brihadrathuriastricht. I know the names are strange, but I knew it wouldn't take long, so I began my investigation, but first, I tried to make the first two parts at home only, but after more research I got bad news that the parts cannot be made at home, and I already wasted one year trying to make those parts.

I first checked the store where I got the old paper, and thankfully, I got the special long wires from the store of my new house.

I thought that I would find all the parts within a week, but... it was not easy. Now, for the batteries, I went to the United States first, and after a year, I thought it was impossible, almost depressed, but one day while walking down the street, I saw a pigeon that couldn't fly, then I noticed a small paper on his leg, which was about hints of where the parts of The Time Machine are kept. I was very happy! But the astonishing thing was that the monuments given in the three hints were in India!

I returned to India, but I had already squandered six years. And I almost forgot about the task for which I came to the US, but thanks to this pigeon, which gave me the hints.

Earlier I thought that the two parts would not be in India, but they were! Then I discovered the two special parts in India; these special parts were in historical monuments in India. The following year was spent correctly assembling the parts and finally building the Time Machine.

TWO

ENTRY IN 2123 (MY HOME)

I got a free house too. I entered through my third-hand refrigerator, which was only the secret door to my time machine. Now, let us go out of this fridge. O! My! God! Is this a kitchen? It was a 2 by 2 room with a big screen, and there was an oven-type box. I opened it, and nothing was there inside. Suddenly, the screen turned on, there were the names of some dishes, and I randomly clicked on one to check what it was. Suddenly, a notification popped up, and it was about $6 that had been debited from my bank account. I was still confused. Suddenly, the oven-type box opened, and there was a non-vegetarian dish, and guess what? I am a vegetarian! My money was wasted.

Now, I opened the door of the kitchen and moved towards the next room, which was my bedroom—small screen again! I pressed the first of four buttons, and the TV popped out of the wall, with the news channel showing the report that life is now possible on Neptune as well!

"Now life is possible on all eight planets," says the news anchor.

I again tap the button, and the TV goes inside the wall. Now I pressed the second button, and boom! My bed came out of the ground. Then, I pressed the third button, and as I pressed it, a table and chair popped out of the ground. As I pressed the fourth button, a new door to the bathroom popped out.

I entered the bathroom and saw a poster with the words "Say shower." I said shower, and water began to flow from the shower. There were more buttons for other functions in the bathroom.

Now, I went outside the bedroom and entered my hall. Everything was normal; nothing was new. Minor changes like automatic curtain, screens in place of switchboards, as I moved further again! I saw a screen... It was the largest of them all. As I saw it, it turned on, and there were several games on the screen, one of which looked familiar (I thought I had played it earlier). I tapped it, and a light flashed in my eyes. Boom! I was in another world in that game. The best game I've ever played appears to be real life, but it was actually real life. I was not playing with the game; the game was playing with me. Now, I was bored, and finally I came out of the game and stepped toward the main gate of my house and opened the gate by using my fingerprint.

THREE
THE WORLD

There was a pair of boots, and as soon as I put them on, I was in the air, floating in the air. Trains and buses were flying like planes, and cars were flying like helicopters without wings. The only reason people went down was to buy something, which means the transportation was going on in the air and the rest of the work was done on the ground. Suddenly, an elderly man with a white beard and greying hair, wearing a yellow badge, approached me and inquired,

"Are you new here?"

"Y..ye.. y.. yes!" I replied

"We invented something a few days ago; take this capsule and go home and have this;

remember, take it only after going home," he said, handing me a capsule.

I was excited after hearing this, so I rushed to my house, entered it, and I was very excited, so I ran towards my bedroom, ate that capsule... the world was shaking, I was not able to feel anything, my heart beat became faster, and suddenly, I felt the worst pain in my stomach; I had never felt such a bad pain, and after 2 minutes, I fainted. After 3 to 4 hours, I woke up and saw the time: 12:30 AM. I went to a clinic nearby, which I saw when I was rushing towards my house. The clinic was having a long line; it was not usual for me to see such a clinic.

When my turn came, I saw a robot. I was again confused and not able to understand anything.

"What is it?" I asked, irritably.

"You have to type the problem you're having into that robot," said the person standing behind me.

I typed my problem, that someone handed me a capsule, which I ate and fainted

As I pressed enter, it was loading, and after some time it displayed an error.

"Try again later," said the person behind me.

"Is there a physical therapist nearby?"

He laughed and ignored me.

I left the place. I saw an old man sitting on a bench in the park and enjoying the games on the screen attached to the bench.

"Sir, I have a problem; I am quite confused."

"But why, boy?"

"Today evening, an old man gave me a capsule, and as I ate it, I fainted," I replied.

He laughed and spoke.

"Oh, it was the brain chip seed," he said.

"But what exactly is it? I've never heard of it."

"It enables you to control things with your mind, but remember, you can only operate personal items," he said.

I was about to leave when I realised, I had forgotten to ask the old man that question.

"What are you doing here?" It's 1:30 AM."

"Nothing; mind your own business," he said rudely. I thanked him and ran away from there.

I entered my house, went to my bed, and slept for under a minute, as I was tired.

Through the capsule that I ate, I was now able to select the dream! But as I was tired, I skipped the dream and slept. The next morning, I woke up, freshened up, and moved towards my hall. I stopped suddenly, because I saw a new door, which was for my wardrobe. As I thought of the outfit, it appeared in front of me. I wore it and *went out to explore more.*

First, I went to a bus station, and the buses were landing and departing like airplanes; the railway station also looked a bit the same, and the trains were also landing on land and departing from there; however, the strangest thing I saw was a... space station.

Then I remembered the news anchor who was discussing life on the eighth planet. There was also the poster depicting the price of tickets, which looked like this:

PLANET TICKET PRICE

Mercury $150 Venus $200 Mars $400 Jupiter $600 Saturn $1000 Uranus $1500 Neptune $2000

The population left on earth was reduced to 1 billion because the rest of the population was shifted to other planets. Then I moved towards the market and entered a snack shop. There was no shopkeeper; there was a robot. I had to select the object we want to buy, and then it will tell you the price. Give the money to the robot, and it will bring you the object you want.

As I already expected, there were self-driving cars, which were normal for the people there. There was no traffic light visible; there was an automatic system, and the cars were interconnected, so when it was necessary, the cars stopped by themselves and there was no traffic. There were two Sundays in a week. People bought robots for their work. Nothing was there like God, festivals, religion, spirituality, etc.

Marriages were the only events held in those days; people invited the entire town to this celebration; people did not even celebrate their birthdays; there was no government; people lived on their own wishes. Restaurants were not there as the automatic kitchens gave them everything they wanted; seven days passed. I was still amazed, and I was exploring things as much as I was able to. After eating the brain chip seed, I was able to click photos and record videos with my eyes. As I blinked my eyes twice, a photo was clicked, and as I blinked my eyes three times, a video recording started.

You have probably heard of holograms... because computers didn't have screens, they were controlled with fingers in the air as hologram technology advanced.

Transport watches were available on the market; however, people mostly used cars; however, the very privileged and rich people used them because they were very expensive. You simply had to click on the location you wanted to go on the maps provided in the watch, and you will be there.

Not only this, but many more advanced technologies were provided in 2123.

FOUR

MY NEW FRIEND

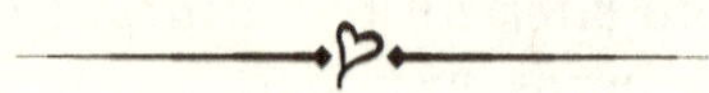

One day, I was walking in the park, and a boy (almost my age) came and asked me,

"Hey! Why are you so weird? I've been noticing you for three days now, and you are acting like you're from another planet?

"What is the problem?" he continued.

"Do you live alone?" I asked him

"Yah," he replied.

"Then I want to tell you a secret." "Don't share it with anyone," I told him.

"What's the secret?"

"I have come from 2023."

He was totally shocked.

"Please accompany me; I'll explain everything," I said and we took off and flew to my house.

"This is my time machine," I told him, pointing towards my old, third-handed refrigerator.

"Ha ha ha ha... what is this?"

"See, I'm not joking," I said, explaining the entire story; he was now serious.

"And after Lightning 2023, I will write a book on my experiences," I said.

And we became friends after this long conversation.

"By the way, what is your name?"

"Ojas," I replied.

"And yours?"

"Sam," he said.

I started exploring with my new friend Sam the next day.

The next day, he came to my house with an iron capsule in his hand.

"What is this?"

"This is how we construct homes nowadays," he replied.

"But how"

He took me to an open place, and then he dug a hole in the ground, put the capsule in it, sprinkled a special gel on it, and ran away from there. I also followed him.

And in the place where the seed or capsule was inserted, a luxury bungalow was constructed in the blink of an eye.

"That's our new house, Ojas!"

"WOW......................" I was amazed

"Did you know that crops and trees can now be grown in less than a second?" he asked.

Sam was an orphan and a scientist.

The capsule that the old man gave was invented by him alone.

FIVE

Exploring with Sam

"Let's go"

"Where????" I asked

"To my lab."

"Oh...." I was excited.

As we reached the lab, I was surprised—his lab was bigger than the airports in the year 2023.

"Do you work here alone?"

"Yes," he replied.

My friend Sam's other well-known invention was... air boots, which are used to fly through the air.

He took out some capsules from his special locker and gave me one.

"Eat it!"

I ate that and felt so energetic!

"It is amripsule."

"But what is it?"

"By eating it, you will never die!"

I was very shocked, and I took three more from him for my family in 2023.

Now Sam took me to a school, the greatest building in the city! As Sam was a great scientist, the school was decorated, and the students were standing on the main gate of the school for Sam's welcome, as he was invited to an event.

"He is a great scientist," people whispered.

We saw the classes; there were no teachers, only robots, robots, and robots. The principal and the helpers were also robots.

There were no blackboards and chalk; teachers taught through holograms! which they operated through their fingers.

The days are flying by, and I am relishing them. I bought a big house soon.

I used to spend entire days out of the house, and the house became filthy. One day, I bought a robot on an e-commerce website, and the delivery was so quick that it arrived at my house in under 3 minutes. The robot was very interactive.

Soon, Sam shifted to Uranus, and he left me alone.

One day, I was walking in a park alone.

I noticed that the gardening was also done by the robots.

I wasn't feeling well because, in 2023,great scientists stated that robots can be dangerous.

However, to live there, I needed money.

So for this, after one to two months, I opened a school named The 2123 School.

I worked hard on it and used very advanced technologies, so my school became the best school in the country within 3 months, and I became a billionaire. As I was now a billionaire and had much money in my house and I also used to stay all days out of my house. The money that I kept became half.

Now, I had hired real security guards, my entire investment was lost the next day, and the guards I had retained were killed, and the situation became dire. I didn't tell anyone that this was happening in my house.

One day I hid in my house and kept some money where I used to keep it earlier. I was shocked because the robots took that money and gave it to a person. The person was a stranger, and I didn't know him. The strange man bought wide batteries for the robots and returned them the rest of the money. When there was not any need for batteries. They also installed the parts like guns, bombs, and many more violent objects and used to hide them in their store box. Then I thought, "Let's see why this man is doing this," and I got to know that he was the only one whom I met in the park and shared my problem with, who told me everything about brain chip seed. And if he himself was a robot, then I understood why he was not going to his home!

SIX

HUMAN V/S ROBOTS

I once bought a robot that looked exactly like me. I sent him toward the rest of the robots and instructed him to say that.

"Hey, robots," I said, "I saw it all, wh..y?"

The robot killed him with the guns, Now I understand why the security guards were died.

The next day I went to the space station and took a spaceship to Uranus and tried to find Sam. In 3 days, I found him and told him everything. He was shocked to hear so

A good thing about other planets was that no robots were used. I and Sam collected 3 billion people from different planets and formed a massive army, but the number of robots on Earth was still higher. We also collected 500 to 1000 aliens from different planets, which may sound strange, but aliens were present.

Our first strategy was to turn off many of the robots, which were divided into two categories: those that could be turned off and those that couldn't.

On the first day, we switched off about 98,000,000 robots, and the good news was that the robots were not interconnected and only became violent when they saw another robot killed.

On the second day, we also switched off about one billion robots; now there were only 2 billion robots left, and we also included the people on earth, which were one billion, so now we were an army of 4 billion people.

On the third day, we started killing them. That day, we killed 30,764 robots, but if we continue at that speed, nothing will happen. We had a conference, and we decided to gather all the robots at 1:00 and kill them in one go, but that was the worst decision ever. On the fifth day, we called all the robots, but they didn't know that we were planning to destroy them. As we shot the first robot, all the other robots disappeared, and they appeared behind us and killed one billion people from our team and the rest when they wreaked havoc.

Thanks to Sam, who was sitting in the control room of his lab and hacked the robots, he could not kill them; however, he switched them off, but only for 30 minutes. All the people shifted to Neptune, and everyone thought that the earth was now the planet of robots. A year passed, and technology had developed so much that a single person was able to kill three robots at one time. But we thought they might have doubled their population because they knew how to make other robots like them.

SEVEN

ROBOTS ON NEPTUNE

And within a month we were about to go to earth. But before that, we also sent teams of people to other planets so that they could teach other people their skills and techniques so that they could help us in times of need.

A week later, a spaceship from Earth was detected; we were all prepared because we knew there were only robots left on Earth, but what surprised us was that there were several robots in the spaceship when it landed, as well as jumbo robots, and as they landed, the Neptune was blasted from their bombs .And as this happened... I woke up and thank God! that it was just a nightmare, but the next day our system actually detected a spaceship from the earth. We decided that we would blast the spaceship in the air only, but Sam suggested that.

"They should not get any idea about the fact that we know their spaceship is landing on Neptune."

And we all agreed, but who knows if that was the worst mistake? We were all prepared when the spaceship touched down. But millions of 15-centimetre camera robots are spread all over Neptune.

"I think they sent these robots to spy on us," I said.

Sam smiled after hearing this, and now I was curious why Sam was behaving like this?

"What should we do now, Sam?" I asked him.

"We cannot do anything," he replied.

I was shocked to hear this type of response from him for the first time.

Now I've started to follow him. I followed him everywhere he went. He went to a control room; I didn't know any control room existed like this. I was trying to see him from outside, and he was watching the view from all the small camera robots on his computer screen!

As there were many robots, one was standing behind me, and Sam was getting the view from it. As Sam saw that, he turned back, and I made him fall from the electric current gun that I was using, and when he woke up, I captured him in a room with other humans.

"Why are you doing this?" I asked

"Wh...what did I do?" he asked.

"don't lie!" I said it in anger.

"I'm a robot, and Sam was kidnapped by other robots on ea. ahh!"

As he said that, the person standing behind me shot him from the gun, and the robot was dead.

On the next day, we killed all the camera robots, and we all went to earth. The good thing was that they were not able to multiply their population. because they could not manage to create batteries. Many of them died because their batteries were not working.

Now we all went to the earth and killed the robots, and only four master mega-huge robots with the highest power were left.

"I think they can't be killed," I said.

The Sam was captured by the mega robots.

"One, two, three!"

As I said that we all ran together towards them. Sam then moved away from them; we were constantly distracting them, and Sam climbed over one robot, he opened his head and changed the programmed system, and Sam directed the robot to kill the other three robots, and by chance, the one left robot's battery had died.

We all celebrated after killing all the robots in the universe; everyone was happy. After a few months, all the robots' jobs and duties were replaced by humans, and the world returned to normalcy, but technology that had not been continued by robots continued to function, and now all the humans from other planets have returned to earth and are living a happy life.

EIGHT

THE ENDING

I and Sam went back to my first house, and I entered my 3rd-hand fridge and saw Sam for the last time with tears in his eyes. Then, when I went back to 2023, I wrote a book on my experiences and published it. However, people still didn't believe, except my family members. Sam declared in 2123 that I am no longer alive and have been killed by any disease; we didn't wanted people to know that I am from 2023, so we lied to them.